# Ark Adventures

Noah and his wife think a flood might be coming, so they have built a big boat called the Ark. They are sailing around the world to rescue the animals before it starts to rain.

*Let's all go on an animal adventure!*

For Poppy Bond
S.G.

For Hamish
A.P.

Reading Consultant: Prue Goodwin, Lecturer in literacy and children's books

ORCHARD BOOKS
338 Euston Road, London NW1 3BH
*Orchard Books Australia*
Level 17/207 Kent Street, Sydney, NSW 2000

First published in 2011
First paperback publication in 2012

ISBN 978 1 40830 556 0 (hardback)
ISBN 978 1 40830 564 5 (paperback)

Text © Sally Grindley 2011
Illustrations © Alex Paterson 2011

A CIP catalogue record for this book is available from the British Library.

1 3 5 7 9 10 8 6 4 2 (hardback)
1 3 5 7 9 10 8 6 4 2 (paperback)

Printed in China

Orchard Books is a division of Hachette Children's Books,
an Hachette UK company.

# Too-slow
## Tortoises!

Written by Sally Grindley
Illustrated by Alex Paterson

ORCHARD BOOKS

It was a fine, sunny day aboard the Ark. "Look at the sign, Noah. We're heading for the Galapagos Islands," said Mrs Noah. "Which animals will we find there?"

Noah opened their *Big Book of Animals.*

"Giant tortoises!" he said. "It says some of them are one hundred and fifty years old!"

"That's older than you!" said Mrs Noah.

"And it says they're *very* slow," added Noah.

They reached the islands and
anchored the Ark.

"I'll stay and feed the other animals, while you find the tortoises," said Mrs Noah.

"Tortoises eat grass," said Noah. "I'll look for grassy places." "Good idea!" said Mrs Noah.

Noah stepped ashore and walked across the island, until at last he came to a big grassy place. "I'm sure tortoises will come here," he said.

Noah sat down to wait beside a huge
rock. The sky was blue and the sun
was warm. It made him feel sleepy.
"I'll just have a quick doze . . ."
he said.

When Noah woke up again, there
was another huge rock close by.

"Strange," he said. "I'm sure that wasn't there before. Now, where are those tortoises?"

He yawned and leant back against
the rock. Suddenly, it began to rise.

"Argh!" squealed Noah. "What's
happening?"

Slowly, a head popped out from
underneath the rock. Two eyes
blinked at him.

"I've found one!" Noah cried.

"I've found a giant tortoise!"

The second rock moved upwards and another head popped out.

"I've found two!" cried Noah. "You do look *very* old," he added. "Would you like a ride on my Ark?"

The tortoises began to walk across the grass towards the Ark.

"Oh dear. You are *very* slow," said Noah.

He ran back to Mrs Noah. "How can we make the tortoises go faster?" he panted. "It will take them days to reach the Ark."

"I have an idea!" Mrs Noah said. "I'll fetch one of our elephants. You fetch our rubber boat, and some lettuce."

As soon as the elephant, the rubber boat and the lettuce were ready, Noah and Mrs Noah set off together.

"They look *much* older than you!" said Mrs Noah when she saw the tortoises.

"They're *very* slow," said Noah. "We'll soon help them go faster," said Mrs Noah.

They laid the rubber boat flat on the grass. Noah put a pile of lettuce in the middle of it.

"Come on now, my tortoise friends," he said. "It's party time!"

The tortoises walked very slowly towards the piles of lettuce.

At last, they began
to munch.

"Now," said Mrs Noah to the elephant. "Let's blow up the boat!"

The elephant put its trunk over the air hole on the boat, and blew.

The rubber boat
began to rise up . . .

. . . and up . . .

"A little more . . ."
said Noah.

The boat rose up and up until Noah
called, "Stop!"
The two tortoises sat inside it,
munching happily on the lettuce.

Noah gently tied a
rope around the
elephant's tummy.

"Off we go, back to the
Ark!" said Mrs Noah.

The strong elephant pulled as hard as he could. The boat began to move across the grass, faster and faster . . .

"I bet you've never moved that fast before," Noah called to the tortoises. Just then he saw that Mrs Noah had jumped up next to them.

"Hey, wait for me!" he cried as he
ran to catch up.

"You're so *very* slow, Noah," laughed
Mrs Noah.

# SALLY GRINDLEY · ALEX PATERSON

Crazy Chameleons!            978 1 40830 562 1

Giant Giraffes!              978 1 40830 563 8

Too-slow Tortoises!         978 1 40830 564 5

Kung Fu Kangaroos!          978 1 40830 565 2

Playful Penguins!            978 1 40830 566 9

Pesky Sharks!               978 1 40830 567 6

Cheeky Chimpanzees!          978 1 40830 568 3

Hungry Bears!               978 1 40830 569 0

All priced at £4.99

Orchard Books are available from all good bookshops, or can be
ordered from our website: www.orchardbooks.co.uk,
or telephone 01235 827702, or fax 01235 827703.